SAM and CHARLIE

(AND SAM TOO)

RETURN!

Leslie Kimmelman   *Illustrated by* William Owl

Albert Whitman & Company
Chicago, Illinois

Library of Congress Cataloging-in-Publication data is on file with the publisher.

Text copyright © 2014 by Leslie Kimmelman
Illustrations copyright © 2014 by Albert Whitman & Company
Published in 2014 by Albert Whitman & Company
ISBN 978-0-8075-7215-3
Printed in China.
10 9 8 7 6 5 4 3 2 1 NP 18 17 16 15 14 13

The design is by Nick Tiemersma.

For more information about Albert Whitman & Company,
visit our web site at www.albertwhitman.com.

To Bernie,
a true friend—L.K.

For Betty—W.O.

TABLE OF CONTENTS

Friendship is man's greatest gift.

–Moses Ibn Ezra

This is Sam.

This is Charlie,
his best friend and
next-door neighbor.

This is Charlie's
little sister. Her
name is Sam Too.

They have lots of fun together.

A SNOWY DAY

On snowy days, Sam helped his neighbors shovel their walks.

Mr. Binder's house was first. Mr. Binder had a bad back.

Charlie tromped by with her shovel. "It'll be easier if I help," she said.

"Okay," said Sam. "But you might get hat hair." He knew that Charlie could be sensitive about her hair.

"That's okay," said Charlie. "All for a good cause."

But Mr. Binder's walk was already finished. "My nephew is visiting," he explained. "Thank you anyway."

The O'Donnells' walk was also done. Someone had been there with a snowblower.

"Using a machine is cheating," said Charlie.

Sam agreed. "*Anyone* can shovel with a machine."

But Mrs. Rosen's walk definitely needed help.

Charlie had said it would be easier with two people. But it wasn't easier. Not with Charlie in front.

Not with Charlie in back either.

When they finally finished, Sam and Charlie both looked like snow people. "At least the walk is clean," said Charlie.

"Only our houses are left," said Sam, and they got right to work. Then...

"Snowball fight?" suggested Sam.

"Snow angels?" suggested Charlie.

"Hot cocoa!" called Sam Too from Charlie's front door. "With whipped cream and sprinkles!"

Charlie's hat hair was a disaster, but the hot cocoa with whipped cream was awesome.

THE TREE'S BIRTHDAY

One wet morning, Sam knocked on Charlie's door.

"Look what the storm did," he said. He pointed to a tree lying on the ground between their two backyards.

Sam Too peeked around Charlie.

"Oh no!" she cried. "That was my favorite tree! Red in the spring, even redder in the fall."

Sam nodded sadly. "It was a great tree."

So Sam, Charlie, and Sam Too had a special ceremony to say good-bye.

"We'll miss you, tree," said Charlie.

"We loved you, tree," said Sam Too.

"Amen," added Sam, because he thought that sounded right.

"Now what?" asked Sam Too.

Sam thought about it. "I have an idea,"

he said. "Meet me here after lunch."

After lunch, Sam was waiting. A big shovel and a pot with a small tree in it were beside him.

"It's Tu B'Shevat, you know," he said.

"Tu B'Sh-what?" asked Sam Too.

"Not Tu-B'Sh*what*. Tu B'She*vat*," Charlie explained. "It's a Jewish holiday that's kind of like a birthday for trees."

"Yep," said Sam. "So my mom and I bought a new tree to plant. It'll grow and grow until it's as big and beautiful as the old tree."

After the tree was in the ground, Sam, Charlie, and Sam Too held hands around it.

"*Happy Birthday to you*," they sang. "*Happy Birthday, dear tree...*"

Then they went inside and all got a piece of chocolate birthday cake. Except for the tree. It just got water.

CRUNCH!

Tonight would be the first night of Passover. Charlie's mom was cleaning the house from top to bottom.

"Let me help," offered Sam Too. She stood up. Breakfast cereal went everywhere. She took a step across the kitchen. *CRUNCH.*

Charlie groaned. "I'll get the broom."

Meanwhile, next door, Sam was helping his mom make haroseth for Seder dinner. The nuts were chopped and the apples were waiting.

"I'm hungry," said Sam.

He took a big bite of apple. CRUNCH.
"Uh-oh!"

"What's the matter?" asked his mom.

"Remember my loose tooth, Mom?" said
Sam. "It's not loose anymore."

Passover was Sam and Charlie's favorite holiday.

At both houses, there were lots of guests: grandparents, aunts, uncles, and cousins.

There was chicken soup with baseball-sized matzah balls.

There was singing at the table—which
was usually not allowed.

And, especially, there was the hunt for
the afikomen before dessert. Someone had to
find the piece of matzah wrapped in a white
napkin and hidden somewhere in the house.

"I'm on a three-year afikomen-finding winning streak," Sam had told Charlie proudly the day before.

"Sweet! What's your secret? At our house, my cousin Freda always finds it," complained Charlie. "I hope this year my luck will change."

When the time came, she looked everywhere.

There was no matzah on the bookshelf. Or under the piano lid. Or behind the computer keyboard.

"Where could it be?"

Charlie wondered. "Where would Sam look?"

She sat in the big armchair to think.

CRUNCH!

"I found the afikomen!" shrieked Charlie—so loudly that Sam, also hunting for the afikomen, heard it all the way from next door.

RAZZAMATAZZ

"Ta-da!" Charlie announced. But Sam wasn't paying attention.

This time, Charlie shouted, "TA-DA!"

Sam looked up.

"Ta-da!" Charlie repeated for the third time. She spun around in the tree house and snapped her fingers. "Your turn."

Sam put down his baseball cards. "*Ta-da?*" he asked.

"You have to do it with razzamatazz," said Charlie.

Sam smiled. If there was one thing he knew, it was razzamatazz.

Sam twirled, flashed his hands, and ended with a huge *TA-DA!* "How's that?"

"Not bad," answered Charlie. "Lots of razzamatazz." She pointed to someone on the sidewalk below. "Hey, who's that?"

"That's Jason," Sam answered.

"How come I haven't met him?" asked Charlie.

"He goes to a different school," said Sam. "And he doesn't talk."

"At all?" asked Charlie.

"Nope," said Sam. "But he smiles a lot."

"Mom says *I* talk enough for two," said Charlie.

Sam climbed down through the red and yellow leaves and back up into the tree house with Jason.

"Charlie, meet my friend Jason. Jason, Charlie," said Sam.

"Hey, Jason, want to see something?" Charlie asked. She and Sam spun around and shouted *ta-da!* "Wanna try?"

Jason looked at his feet. He tapped his toes. Then he spun around and around—and *around*. He clapped his hands and flopped down, a tiny smile on his face. He high-fived Sam with one hand and Charlie with the other.

"Awesome!" said Charlie.

Sometimes the best razzamatazz has no words at all.

THE HANUKKAH QUEEN

It was the last night of Hanukkah. Sam and his family were celebrating with Charlie and her family.

First they had a dreidel contest.

Plop! Charlie's dreidel fell first.

"Keep going, keep going, keep going," whispered Sam Too to her dreidel.

Plop! Sam's dreidel fell.

"I win! I win!" exclaimed Sam Too. She smiled from ear to ear.

Next Sam, Charlie, and Sam Too guessed
which candle would last the longest.

Sam's blue candle burned out first.

"Keep going, keep going," whispered Sam
Too to her candle. But things didn't look
good. The pink candle was melting fast.

Charlie looked over at her sister. Then
she coughed softly—close by her own candle.
Oops! It sputtered and went dark.

Sam Too was very excited. "I win! I win again!" she exclaimed.

Finally it was dinnertime.

"I bet I can eat the most latkes and applesauce," said Sam Too.

"You're on," said Charlie and Sam.

Charlie stopped after three. "I'm full."

Sam and Sam Too ate latke number four.

Sam eyed a fifth. He was still hungry.
He looked at Charlie and then at Sam Too.

Sam Too was anxious. She was little.
She was munching latke number five and
whispering to herself, "I just *have* to win."

Sam moaned. "That's all for me," he said. "I couldn't eat another bite."

Sam Too jumped up. She pumped her fist. "I win! I win for the third time," she squealed.

Sam and Charlie bowed deeply. "Long live Sam Too, the Hanukkah Queen!"